HORSE DIARIES
· Elska ·

HORSE DIARIES

#1: Elska

#2: Bell's Star

HORSE DIARIES

Elska

CATHERINE HAPKA

illustrated by RUTH SANDERSON

RANDOM HOUSE NEW YORK

Text copyright © 2009 by Catherine Hapka
Illustrations copyright © 2009 by Ruth Sanderson

Photo credits: © Arctic Images/CORBIS (p. 108);
© Jay Dickman/CORBIS (p. 106); © Werner Forman/CORBIS (p. 104);
© Quevaal/Dreamstime.com (p. 113); © Sugarfree.sk/Dreamstime.com (p. 110).

Published in the United States by Random House Children's Books,
a division of Random House, Inc., New York.

Random House and colophon are registered trademarks of Random House, Inc.

Visit us on the Web! www.randomhouse.com/kids

Educators and librarians, for a variety of teaching tools, visit us at
www.randomhouse.com/teachers

Library of Congress Cataloging-in-Publication Data
Hapka, Cathy.
Elska / by Catherine Hapka ; illustrated by Ruth Sanderson. — 1st ed.
p.   cm. — (Horse diaries)
Summary: Around the year 1000, the Icelandic horse named Elska is born
and learns about life and her role in the herd, as well as love and friendship,
when she rescues the girl to whom she originally belonged.
Includes facts about Icelandic horses and Iceland.
ISBN 978-0-375-84732-5 (trade) — ISBN 978-0-375-94677-6 (lib. bdg.)
1. Iceland pony—Juvenile fiction. 2. Iceland—History—To 1262—
Juvenile fiction. [1. Iceland pony—Fiction. 2. Horses—Fiction.
3. Iceland—History—To 1262—Fiction.] I. Sanderson, Ruth, ill. II. Title.
PZ10.3.H2258 El 2009 [Fic]—dc22 2007022109

Printed in the United States of America
20 19 18 17 16 15 14

First Edition

For Lisa, the Icelandic expert in the family.

—C.H.

For my models—Hannah, Eli, Evan, Brendan,
David, and Bill. And a special thank-you
to Brian Puntin and the beautiful Icelandic horses
at Roberts Woods Farm, and to Bill Short and
Hurstwic.org for photos of Iceland and research
materials on the Viking age.

—R.S.

CONTENTS

"Oh! if people knew what a comfort to horses a light hand is . . ."

—from *Black Beauty*, by Anna Sewell

HORSE DIARIES
· Elska ·

Iceland, Circa AD 1000

My name is Elska. That is what the people call me, though in the first months of my life I knew nothing of people.

I was foaled in early summer, in a meadow dotted with flowers. My first memory was the feeling of the warm sun on my back. I did not know it then, but in summer in Iceland, the sun shines for more than twenty hours each day. My dam, Silfra, was on her feet within moments of my birth. She nudged at me with her soft muzzle. The scent of her surrounded me and made me feel safe.

My long legs twitched. They felt new and strange. I moved them, trying to figure out how they worked. Finally I got my two front legs out in front and my back legs under me. I gave a push and staggered to my feet.

I swayed back and forth and almost fell. Then I found my balance. I stood on my shaky legs. My brushy tail swished behind me, and my ears twitched at the sounds of my brand-new world. I opened my eyes wide, trying to understand the things I saw. Interesting smells drifted past my nostrils.

My dam nudged me again with her nose, almost tipping me over. I realized I was hungry. I searched along her body until I found the right spot. Then I nursed, the warm milk filling my belly.

Soon I was full, which made me very sleepy. I allowed my new legs to collapse under me, and was asleep almost before I hit the ground.

When I awoke, I stood and nursed again. Energy coursed through my body, and I turned away from my dam. I noticed other creatures nearby—horses like me.

Curious, I tried to run to them. But my long legs tangled with each other and I went sprawling face-first on the ground.

My dam was amused. *Patience, little one,* she told me. *Soon you will be running like the wind.*

Wise Silfra was right. Within hours I was running and playing as if I had been doing so forever. The others welcomed me to the herd.

I met Bergelmir, the herd stallion and my sire. I also met an older filly known as Leira; her patient old dam, Irpa; a sweet filly the humans would call Tyrta, who was only a few days older than I was; and a playful colt with a colorful pinto coat who would be called Tappi.

It was Tappi who first showed me how to tölt. I already knew how to trot and gallop. I could walk, too, though I did it as little as possible—it was too slow when there was so much to do and see! When I first noticed Tappi, he was moving in a different way. His legs flashed beneath him, one-two-three-four, while his head and back stayed straight and proud.

I galloped after him, curious. *Why do your legs move like that?* I wanted to know.

He lifted his knees higher, showing off as he tölted around me. *All the horses of this land can do it,* he told me. *It is called a tölt, and it is what makes us special among all the animals.*

How do you know so much about it? I wanted to know. *You aren't much older than me.*

My mother, Perta, told me, Tappi said. *She is the oldest mare in the herd. She knows everything!*

I watched his legs carefully. Then I tried to make my own move in the same way. After a few tries, I got it. I was tölting! Before long it felt as easy as breathing. My hind legs stretched under my body, one at a time, pushing me forward. My front legs lifted and curled, helping to propel me along. One-two-three-four, one-two-three-four, faster and faster. Tölting was fun!

A few days after my foaling, the rest of the herd left my birth meadow. I kept pace easily, sometimes walking or trotting and sometimes tölting with Tappi. We forded a fast, cold, shallow river that tumbled down from the mountains in a series of waterfalls. Then we climbed a steep, mossy hill and found ourselves overlooking a green valley. A herd of smaller creatures dotted the slopes of the valley and nibbled at the grass. They were white, gray, black, and brown—almost as many colors as there were in my herd. My mother told me that such creatures were known as sheep.

They share our summer grazing lands, she told me. *In autumn, the men come and round them up, along with us.*

I didn't understand all of what she told me. *Summer*, *autumn*, and *men* meant nothing to me. But I didn't let it worry me. Like the way my legs worked, I figured these things would become clear in time.

The herd continued through the valley of the sheep. On the far side, we found ourselves in the shadow of a mountain. Its iron-gray slopes stretched up toward the blue sky. Near the top, veins of silvery white trickled down, like the strands of my friend Tyrta's creamy mane and tail against the dark golden palomino color of her body.

The wise old mare Irpa saw me looking. *That is ice and snow, little one,* she told me. *You will learn more of that soon enough.*

I wanted to know more *now,* but the herd was on the move again. We traveled through more valleys, across high meadows and lava fields, past hot springs and geysers, and over rocky foothills coated with moss. By late evening, when the sun set for the first time in many hours, we reached a broad, grassy plain with a river running through it. Most of the horses waded into the river, drinking deeply. I nursed from my mother, then collapsed onto the soft ground and slept.

That was the first of many journeys I made with the herd. We moved around often in search of grazing. Several months passed and I grew bigger, faster, and stronger. I drank less of my dam's milk and nibbled more grass with the older horses. I grew taller and stouter, and a layer of fat covered my ribs.

Then one day in early autumn, something different happened. Tappi was the first to notice.

New horses! He came running toward the herd, breathless. *Come and see!*

Before we could move, horses crested the next hill. But what was that upon their backs?

Ah, it is Hamur! My dam, Silfra, snorted with pleasure. Her ears were pricked forward

and her gaze trained on a particular roan horse. *See how big he has grown since winter!*

All around me, the other adult horses were expressing similar things. The other foals were just as confused as I was. What was happening?

Still, watching the reaction of my elders,

I knew it could be nothing frightening. The horses came closer, and I got a better look at the odd creatures that rode upon their backs. They sat upright like a bird does, or an arctic fox when it stands on its hind legs to scan the fields. But these creatures were much larger than a fox. They also made strange noises as they came, sharper than the soft snorts and nickers of a horse and louder than the calls of most birds. I cocked my head to listen to these cries.

One was tall with a loud voice: "Watch, Amma! You must stay close to us, or you will not be allowed on the *rettir* again until you are older."

A smaller one responded, "But I am old enough, Jarl! I am nearly eight."

Yet another's voice was like the low rumble of a geyser: "Your brother speaks the truth, Amma. Keep your horse near mine."

"Yes, Father. Ooh! Look at the pretty silver dapple filly over there."

I was trying to puzzle out what the sounds might mean. Then I noticed that the smallest of the odd new creatures was staring straight at me. I took a step closer, curious.

Come, little one. Silfra walked toward me, moving her head to show me which way she wanted me to go. *We are meant to go with the humans now.*

Sure enough, the herd was already drifting

ahead of the newcomers toward the nearest mountain pass. Silfra's body blocked my view for a moment. But when I turned my head to look behind me, the small creature—a *human*, my dam had called it—was still gazing after me.

In the Farmyard

The farmyard was a flat area of hard-packed dirt between a grassy field and a wide, fast-flowing river. In the middle of the yard was a long, low, turf-roofed building with several smaller structures near it. A column of smoke spiraled out of the top of the main building, though it smelled nothing like the sulfur gasps of the volcanoes or the steam of the geysers. Several horses I didn't recognize grazed in a field nearby.

At the time, I understood little of what I saw. Later, I would learn more. The biggest structure was where the humans lived. They grew no thick winter coat like horses, sheep, and dogs did. Instead they huddled inside their houses, heated by fires, wrapped in woolen garments.

I also came to understand better what role we horses played in the life of the humans—and they in ours. For the warm season, most of the family's sheep and some of their horses were turned loose to graze wherever we could find forage. We mingled

with the livestock of neighboring families—
for instance, I discovered that three of the
mares of our herd belonged with another
human family from across the river, and several more went to a different homestead
some distance away. At the start of the season of cold, ice, and snow, all the neighbors
rounded us up—horses and sheep alike—
separated us out, and brought us into the
farmyards for safekeeping.

We had barely arrived when I saw several horses tölt into the yard. A human sat
astride one, while the others carried large
packs strapped to their backs.

*Will I carry people or other loads on my
back someday?* I wanted to know.

Silfra lowered her head and breathed

into my nostrils fondly. *Indeed you will, little one. But not yet. You are still too young.*

"Silfra!" The young human I'd seen earlier slid down from the horse she was riding. She ran toward us, and I was so surprised that I thought my eyes would bug out of my head. She moved on two legs! It was very odd to see—like a bird without wings. But this odd way of moving seemed to come as naturally to her kind as the gallop or tölt did to a horse.

The young human ran right up to my dam and threw her arms around her neck. Silfra lowered her head, nuzzling the girl's hair, which was the soft golden color of a field of dried grasses.

This is the smallest foal of the human family,

she told me. *She is known as Amma. She is very kind to all the horses.*

I crowded close to my mother's flank, watching Amma curiously. She noticed me standing there, and the corners of her mouth turned up. Her smooth skin was nearly as pale as Leira's cremello coat, but her mouth was ruddy and her eyes were the color of the clear sky.

"Is this your latest foal, Silfra? She's beautiful!"

Just then one of the larger humans walked up behind Amma. This one was a male, with light-colored fur covering much of his face and head.

"Found your favorite mare, did you, Amma?" His voice was deeper than the young one's. "Looks like Silfra has given us a silver dapple foal this year. A filly, is it?"

"Yes, Father." Amma looked up at the older human. "I want to call her Elska."

She looked over at me as she pronounced the last word. *Elska*. It stuck in my head. Elska. Elska. Elska.

She has given you a name, little one, Silfra told me proudly. *From now on, you will be known as Elska.*

And so I was. Before long I learned to pick out my name from the humans' speech. A few more of their words became familiar, too—*get over, stand, hay*, and others. But mostly I could tell what they wanted by the way they moved or looked at me. It was easy to please them if I paid attention.

After a brisk, pleasant autumn came the long, cold, dark winter. The sun that spent so much time overhead during the summer months now hid below the horizon for most of the day. We huddled together for warmth, our tails to the wind and icicles forming on our whiskers. The humans brought us dried grass to eat and fresh water to drink. My coat had grown in thick and long, and I only shivered on the very coldest and windiest of nights.

One day, when most of the ice and snow had melted, the humans separated out a number of the horses and tied them apart from the rest of us. I was surprised to see that Silfra was among them. She explained that it was time for the herd to go free again. But this time she would not be coming with us back to the meadows and foothills.

It is my turn to stay and help the humans this warm season, she told me. *You must go with the others to eat grass and grow beneath the summer sun. I will see you again when the days grow shorter.*

Just then Tappi ran up to me. He had grown taller and sturdier over the winter, though he was a bit thin. We all were from the hard season—including the humans.

Tappi snorted at me, his eyes bright and eager. *Come, Elska! The humans have opened the gate. Let's race.*

He didn't wait for an answer before taking

off at a brisk tölt. He broke to a canter as he cleared the gate, and a moment later, he slid into an even faster gait—a flying pace.

I cast one last glance at my dam. Then I took off after Tappi, doing my best to catch up.

3

Three and a Half Years Later

More seasons passed. I was getting used to the pattern of life. When it grew colder and many of the wild birds took flight for warmer lands, we went to the farmyard. When the days lengthened and the birds began to reappear, we returned to the meadows and glaciers and crystal-cold rivers of the open land.

Now it was turning to winter again. Tappi, Leira, Tyrta, and I were nearly fully grown. We helped the new foals understand when the humans showed up to herd us back to the farm.

Among the humans was Amma. She was riding Irpa, who had stayed behind on the farm this past summer. The human girl had grown, just as I had. But her hair was the same bright color, and her eyes just as blue.

"Elska!" she called when she spotted me. She rode toward me. I had learned to read the humans' expressions, and I could tell she was pleased to see me. I was pleased to see her, too, and walked to meet her. She leaned over to give me a scratch on the crest of my neck, her fingers digging down through my thick, bushy mane to find the itchiest spots.

But there was little time for that. Soon her father and brothers and neighbors were shouting for her. Then we, along with the sheep, were setting out on the long trip back to the farmyard.

Once we were settled in, Amma came to visit me. She cooed my name and looked me over, running her hands all along my body. Once again, she seemed pleased by what she saw. I was now as tall as my dam, perhaps even a little taller. My silvery pale mane fell halfway down my neck, and my tail nearly brushed the ground behind me. There were dapples on my rich, dark coat from the months of good forage.

"What are you doing out here?" Amma's eldest brother, Valdi, asked as he appeared in the yard. "Playing with the horses?"

"Elska is old enough to begin training now," Amma answered him. "Father said I can help."

I could sense the excitement in her voice, though I didn't understand her words. Soon after that, my training began. Amma taught me to carry a bit in my mouth and weight on my back. At first it all felt very strange. But I trusted Amma and knew that she meant me no harm, so I tried to do as she asked me. Before long she was riding me across the broad meadows and fording the swift-flowing river to carry messages or small items to neighboring farms. I enjoyed these outings, especially when she talked or sang to me as I trotted or tölted along. Sometimes we would meet her young friends on their horses, and then we would race—I was good at the flying pace, a gait that was faster than trot or tölt, and I often won these races, even when the other horses were older and more experienced. I could tell that this pleased Amma, and so I always tried my hardest. Occasionally one of Amma's brothers would ride me to the shoreline to go fishing or on some other errand. Once or twice, their father or grandfather rode me around the farm. But mostly it was me and Amma exploring the stark autumn lands of Iceland, at least until the days grew too short for much travel.

One not-too-cold day in very early spring, after most of the thick ice was gone from the river but well before the humans began to gather the wool from the sheep, Amma and I rode out to one of the fields.

The sheep were at the far end, near the river, grazing on the soft green shoots of early-spring grasses. Her brother Valdi was with us on a fine, young horse named Jarpur. The humans talked as they rode toward the sheep at a fast tölt.

"You have done a good job with that mare's training," Valdi said.

"It is Elska that has done a good job," Amma said, giving me a scratch on the withers. "She is the smartest and best horse I've ever known. The prettiest, too!"

I briefly pricked my ears at the sound of my name. But I had just noticed something more interesting than the humans' speech. A horse I recognized from the summers,

Haddingur, the stallion from a different herd, was approaching from the direction of the river. A tall human was riding him.

I let out a nicker, as did Jarpur. Haddingur lifted his head and snorted in return.

"Greetings, Alfvaldr," Amma's brother called to the stallion's rider. He sounded very respectful. I wondered if it was because Haddingur was such a fine stallion. "What brings you to our lands?"

"I noticed the glorious coloring of your sister's mare from across the river and hoped for a better look." The tall man dismounted from his horse. He walked over and gave me a pat.

"She looks to be an obedient mount with

a fine tölt," he said to Amma. "Does she pace as well?"

"Oh yes!" Amma sounded proud. "She is the fastest horse on our farm."

She urged me into a flying pace. I responded eagerly, speeding away from the others and then back again. Even though there was no other horse racing me, I went as fast as I could just for the fun of it.

"Very nice," Alfvaldr said when we stopped. "Do you mind if I ride back to the house with you? I would like a few words with your father."

"Of course, sir," Valdi said. "We can go right now."

I had nearly forgotten the meeting an

hour or two later as I dozed in the farmyard with the herd. Then I saw Alfvaldr riding out on Haddingur. Amma and her father were on foot beside him. Amma was crying.

Moments later, Alfvaldr was ponying me away on a lead line. I didn't understand why, but I went with him. That was what Amma had trained me to do.

"You can come visit her if you like, child," Alfvaldr said, pausing beside Amma and her father.

"Thank you again for your kind help with the land dispute between myself and Bergsveinn," Amma's father said to Alfvaldr. "The gift of this fine mare is the least I can do to repay you."

Alfvaldr bowed his head, then gave a tug

on my rope and rode off. I followed along with his horse but cocked an ear behind me, worried by the sad sound of Amma's sobs. But before long we were halfway across the big, dry field on the far side of the house and I could hear her no more.

At the Homestead of Alfvaldr

The farm of Alfvaldr was larger than the one I had just left. Otherwise, it looked much the same. A long, low building housed the humans, and many sheep and horses were in the surrounding fields, along with cattle and even a few pigs.

A tall, lanky boy came running out to greet us. "What have we here, Father?" he cried. "Is that the mare I noticed in the *rettir?*"

"Indeed it is, Magni," Alfvaldr said. "A gift to our family from our neighbors. And you were correct—she is fast."

I didn't understand why I was here. Alfvaldr's mount, Haddingur, sensed my confusion.

My master is important among the men, he told me in his dignified way. *He receives gifts of many horses and other animals. You will live with us now.*

I still didn't understand. My home was on the other side of the river with Amma, Silfra, Tappi, Tyrta, and the others. Why would I live here?

Magni took the lead line from his father.

He looked me over and seemed pleased.

"May I try her, Father?" he asked.

"Of course, my son." Alfvaldr watched

from atop Haddingur as Magni vaulted onto my back.

His legs were longer than even Valdi's. He sat easily, asking me with those long legs to walk forward, and then trot.

He spent a few minutes putting me through my slower paces. When he pushed me into a flying pace, he let out a happy cry. Encouraged by his pleasure, I sped up even more. We crossed the nearest open field in a matter of seconds, then turned around and returned just as quickly.

Alfvaldr had a smile on his face. "She suits you, Magni. Enjoy her."

"I will!" Magni sounded breathless. "With this mare, I will never lose a race again!"

A little later, I found myself with

Alfvaldr's herd. There were three or four mares there who sometimes ran with my herd during the summers, and they greeted me and helped me settle in among the others. Magni came once to see me, along with some other humans. They all patted me kindly.

But by the time the long, dim twilight was half over, I was growing restless. I thought of my familiar herd and wanted to be with them. I wanted to see Amma as well. I missed the musical sound of her voice and the way she always found the itchiest spots on my crest and withers.

Thank you for helping me, I told the mares from my herd. *I will see you again when summer arrives.*

Then I jumped over the low stone wall
keeping us in and started running across the
next field.

My instincts told me which way to go. I chose a shorter route than the one Alfvaldr had taken. Instead of looping around through flat, open fields, I crossed a rocky area filled with moss and went down a steep hill covered with scree. This brought me to the river at a deep but narrow spot.

I plunged into the water. It was icy cold with the melt from faraway mountaintops and glaciers, but I didn't mind. On the far bank I shook myself dry, then continued on my way.

The other horses heard or smelled me coming from some distance away. Their nickers of greeting caused me to speed up from a trot to a tölt. When I arrived, I saw Amma standing among the horses with her arms around Silfra's neck and tears on her face.

She gasped when she saw me. "Elska! You're back!" she yelled. She flung herself at me and buried her face in my mane. I don't think she even noticed that it was still damp from the river crossing.

I looped my neck down around her and snuffled into her ear. It was good to be home.

5

Back and Forth

I was dozing in the farmyard the next morning when I heard angry voices. It was Alfvaldr. Magni was with him, along with a boy only slightly bigger than Amma. The others called this smaller boy Tassi. The name reminded me of my herdmate Tappi, and the boy reminded me of him, too. Though one was a horse and one human, their eyes held the same playful look.

"Where is my horse?" Alfvaldr roared, swinging down from his stallion's back.

Around me, the herd stirred uneasily. The anger of humans is a fearsome thing. Nearby, the sheep whirled in a panic and ran away.

Magni hurried into the yard and spotted me. "You were right, Father!" he yelled. "She is here!"

Amma's father emerged from the house. "What is all the noise out here?" he cried. "Oh, Alfvaldr! I did not expect your visit."

"What else would you expect?" Magni asked. "You stole back my mare!"

Amma and her brothers emerged from the house.

"What?" Jarl cried. "My father didn't steal anything!"

"My son speaks the truth." Amma's father puffed out his chest. "How dare you accuse me of stealing!"

Alfvaldr pointed toward me. "How dare I? The proof stands there on four hooves!"

"I am telling you, I had nothing to do with it!" Amma's father said.

"It's true!" Amma's voice sounded very small among the angry men. "Elska came back on her own—last night. She missed me."

Her father rounded on her, looking startled. "And you did not tell me this, daughter?" he exclaimed. "Are you trying to cause a blood feud between Alfvaldr and me?"

"No, Father!" Amma started to cry. "Of course not! But Elska is my horse!"

Alfvaldr's younger boy, Tassi, looked confused. "I thought Elska was ours," he said to his father.

"She became mine when she was gifted to me." Alfvaldr's face was hard. He dropped a hand onto Tassi's shoulder but kept his eyes on Amma's father. "I take that seriously, neighbor."

"As do I, neighbor." Amma's father raised both hands in a calming way. "Please accept my apology for this inconvenience. Of course you will have your mare back. Along with another horse of your choice, three of my finest sheep, and a pup from my best dog's next litter."

Alfvaldr stroked his chin. "It is done," he

said. "Come, boys. You can help me choose
our new horse."

Amma was still crying. She took a step

toward me. But her brother Valdi grabbed her by the shoulder and pulled her back into the house.

I arrived back at Alfvaldr's homestead along with Leira and several sheep. But I was not worried. Why should I be? I could jump the fence and be home again that night.

But the other horses cautioned me. They were wiser than I was in the ways of humans. An older mare named Faxa tried to help me understand.

The humans have their odd ways, she explained. *In the summer, they allow some of us to wander free. But in the cold months, they want all of us to stay where they enclose us. This I have learned in my many years.*

But my home is with my herd, and with

Amma, I protested. *Why should I not return
there?*

Faxa lowered her head. *It is for Amma's
sake that you should not,* she told me. *Your leav-
ing made Alfvaldr angry with your other humans.
That is not good for your Amma.*

6

Training Time

I stayed with Alfvaldr's family through that spring. Magni and his brother Tassi continued my training with help from their father. They rode me all over their lands. Sometimes they ponied me from another horse, and other times they rode me and ponied others. I helped prepare the fields for the hay harvest and collect the sheep for the wool gathering. Tassi rode me to carry messages to other homesteads, and Magni often raced me against the horses of friends and neighbors. All of it was interesting, though the races were perhaps my favorite. I often won by a good margin, which pleased Magni and earned me extra pats.

The family treated me well. Even gruff Alfvaldr often had a kind word for me. The other horses accepted me. But still I missed my first home, my old herd, and my Amma.

At least I would soon see the old herd. When summer came, I planned to find them and stay with them until the next *rettir*.

But when the day came to turn us loose,

I got a surprise. Magni and his father pulled out the horses that were to stay behind for the summer. And I was among them!

I tugged against the rope as the others galloped off for the open lands. But I did not pull very hard. To do so was against my training. Still, I could not help feeling unhappy for a while.

But soon I got used to this new way of life, too. Sometimes I would spend a whole summer day lazing about the field. Other times I was busy almost from sunup to sundown. My work was varied and interesting. For instance, there was one time when Magni came running out to find me, his eyes wide and excited.

"Come, Elska!" he cried, vaulting onto my back. "We must fetch the midwife. The baby is coming today!"

We rode quite a long way at a very fast pace. On the way back, a woman rode me as fast as I could go, while Magni followed on a different horse.

I was tired when we got back. After eating for a while, I lay down for a nap. I awoke some time later to loud, shrill, strange cries. When I opened my eyes, I saw Alfvaldr grinning down at me. He held a strange bundle in his arms. The cries were coming from the bundle.

"Good work today, Elska!" he exclaimed. "Say hello to my new daughter, Sunnifa!"

I snuffled at the bundle. It smelled some-
what like a human. Then I understood. This
was a new human foal!

I wasn't sure why Alfvaldr had brought it
to me. But I snorted at it with interest. He

laughed and pulled the baby away, then hurried back into the house.

On other days there were different tasks for me to do. Sometimes I stayed on the farm, where I might be called upon to round up the sheep, help with the crops, or drag a rock out of a field. Other times I went out and about across the countryside. I might carry one of the humans to a neighboring homestead, haul a bundle of goods here or there, or carry a load of fish home from the big river. Through it all, I did my work as best I could. I still missed my old home and old friends. But I tried not to worry over it. After all, as Faxa and the others liked to remind me, such is the life of a horse.

The *Rettir*

The bright days grew shorter and the twilight longer and cooler. My coat thickened and the birds began to disappear. It was autumn again.

Soon it would be time for the *rettir*. This was an important time for the humans. It was when they gathered and sorted their grazing livestock and brought them closer to home for the winter.

But it was also important for other reasons. Everyone in the area worked together. The humans got to visit with their neighbors and catch up on news. It was a time for enjoyment as well as work.

Before this I was always one of the horses being gathered. This year I found that I would be helping with the gathering.

One brisk morning Magni came to get me. His young brother, Tassi, was with him and selected Faxa as his mount. Their father soon appeared and chose his usual mount, Haddingur.

"Come, boys," Alfvaldr said, sounding

more cheerful than usual. "It is time for the *rettir*!"

We set out across the meadows at a brisk tölt. Before long we reached an area of rough volcanic terrain. But all of us horses had grown up with such footing and had no trouble. Soon after that, we met up with neighbors from downriver and rode on together.

"Nice horse, Magni," one of the newcomers said. "Did you breed her from your mare Faxa?"

"No, she was a gift to my father," Magni said. "We call her Elska. She can beat any horse around in a race."

I flicked an ear back at the sound of my

name. Magni leaned forward to give me a pat.

"I can show you her flying pace if you like," he said to the others.

"No, you cannot," Alfvaldr said sternly. "We have much riding ahead of us. There is no sense tiring your horse with foolishness."

I could feel Magni shrug by the way his seat moved on my back. "All right, Father," he said. "The rest of you will have to wait to see what my horse can do."

The humans continued chatting as we moved on. After a while, we reached a flat area where other horses and riders were gathered. Beyond on a grassy hillside I could see a large herd of sheep.

We set to work, circling around to gather up all of the sheep. Magni and I worked hard together. I was proud to know that I was helping.

The silly sheep sometimes tried to run off, but we kept them moving in the right direction. They rushed down the hill and through a channel between two mountains.

On the other side of the pass, we found more riders waiting. One of them was my Amma! I recognized her right away by her scent and the sound of her voice. But her appearance had changed. She was taller now, and her hair was even lighter. She was riding Tyrta, the gentle-natured palomino mare foaled the same summer as I. By the easy way Amma sat Tyrta's trot, I could tell they were doing well together.

I let out a snort as I came closer. Amma

looked up. She recognized me, and for a moment her expression showed joy.

But then she burst into tears. Yanking Tyrta's head around, she took off across the meadow at a brisk gallop.

8

A Reunion and an Accident

I was confused and saddened by Amma's odd behavior. Would I ever truly understand humans?

There was no time to worry over it at that moment. Magni and I still had a lot of work to do.

Later, it was finally time for a rest. We had reached one of the holding pens and driven the sheep inside. Magni left me with the other horses in a grassy area near the edge of the big river. Then he went to do human things with the others gathered nearby.

I saw that Tyrta and several others from my old herd were already grazing in the grassy area. They greeted me as I wandered over and dropped my head to graze near them. I was tired and hungry and it felt good to have a rest.

Do your new humans treat you well, Elska? Tyrta wanted to know.

They do, I told her. *There is good grazing at their farm, and fresh, cool water.*

We were still grazing a short while later

when I heard human footsteps, soft and quick. I cast my gaze back and saw that it was Amma.

"Elska!" she cried, rushing forward.

A moment later, her arms were around my neck. Her familiar scent filled my nostrils as I nuzzled at her hair. She was taller, but otherwise, she was mostly the same.

She hugged me tightly. "I've missed you so much," she said into my neck. "Why did you have to be the one to go? Why did stupid Alfvaldr have to notice you?"

I rested my chin on her shoulder. It was good to be with her again.

Finally Amma loosened her grasp. She looked around at the other horses grazing nearby.

"My father warned me not to come," she

said softly. "He is afraid of angering Alfvaldr. But I'm not afraid of anyone, chieftain or not."

She sounded almost angry. I blinked at her, a little confused by her sudden shift in mood.

A second later, she was happy again. She moved to my side and vaulted onto my back. She weighed a little more than before, but quite a bit less than Magni. Her seat and legs still felt familiar.

"One quick ride," she whispered, nudging me into an easy tölt. "Nobody has to know. . . ."

We rode to the bank of the river, then turned south and followed its path downstream. The sun was still shining, and my earlier weariness was gone. Carrying Amma didn't feel like work. It was more like playing with Tappi and Tyrta and Leira when we were all foals together.

We slowed to a walk for a while, and she leaned forward, hugging me from above. "Oh, Elska," she said with a sigh. "I wish we could run away together. Then you would never have to go back to Alfvaldr."

I heard sadness in her voice. Turning my head, I nudged at her foot with my muzzle. I did not like my Amma to be sad.

We rode on for a while in silence. Finally Amma let out a sigh.

"We'd better go back," she said. "If any-one notices we're gone . . ."

We turned back to return to the others. We were almost there when a shout rang out.

"Hey! What are you doing on my brother's horse?"

It was Tassi. He was staring at us from among the other horses.

Amma gasped. Spinning me around, she kicked me into a gallop. We raced downstream

again until we were out of sight behind a craggy volcanic outcropping.

"Oh no," she moaned, sliding down from my back. "That was Alfvaldr's son. He will tell his father what I was doing!" She gave me a hug. "Go back to the others, Elska," she commanded. "I'm going to run home on my own. If I cross the river here, I know a short-cut. That way, perhaps Father will be too tired to punish me by the time he gets home from the *rettir*."

I didn't understand her words, but it was easy to understand the slap she gave me on the rump. I took a few steps forward and glanced back. She waved her hands to shoo me on. Although I did not want to leave her, I did as she asked.

But horses' eyes are on the sides of our heads rather than the front. That means we can easily see what is happening well behind us. So I was watching when Amma waded into the fast-moving river, wincing and hugging herself as the cold water splashed around her legs.

And I was also able to see when she reached a deeper spot and slipped on the slick rocks. She jerked backward with a cry and disappeared under the foamy, racing water.

9

The Rescue

Amma is in danger!

The idea filled my mind. My training
told me to continue on as she had commanded. But my instincts said otherwise—
and they were much stronger. Spinning
around, I raced toward the bank of the river.

I plunged into the icy-cold water without pausing. It swirled around my legs, and a chunk of ice bounced off my fetlock.

Halfway across the river, Amma popped to the surface. She waved her arms and cried out.

"Amma!" a voice yelled from the shore. It was Tassi. He had followed us just in time to see Amma's fall. He turned and ran away, but I did not worry about that. All my focus was on Amma.

The water was sweeping her downstream. She grabbed for a rock that jutted out and clung to it. Her feet and legs swept out before her, but she held on with all she had. How much longer would her strength last?

I plowed on through the current. It dragged at my legs. Soon it was up to my

withers. The effort and the cold made my muscles ache, but I kept on without pausing.

Amma saw me. "Elska!" she cried out. Her small hands gripped the rock. I could see her arms tremble.

The water tried to push me downstream. But it was not strong enough. I had made similar crossings many times, either moving with the herd or carrying humans. There are many rivers in this country, and very few bridges. We horses are the bridges of Iceland.

Growing up in the rocky volcanic terrain had made me sure-footed and nimble. Living with the elements had made my legs and body strong and able to withstand terrible cold. My hard hooves found purchase among the slippery rocks. I pushed on against the current and the chill. Behind me, I still heard shouting. But I no longer paid it any mind.

Finally I reached Amma. She stared at me with terror in her eyes.

I moved around her as carefully as I could, not wanting to jar her loose from the safety of the rock. Then I was directly beside her, blocking the worst of the current. I lowered my head toward her. Would she know what to do?

She did. Letting go of the rock, she grabbed for me. The current snaked under my belly and tried to sweep her away. But her hand caught a thick strand of my damp mane and hung on.

I braced against the water, trying not to move. Amma scrabbled at my withers with her other hand. Her legs drifted out behind her, and for a moment I feared the current would take her away. But finally she found a chunk of mane there as well. She pulled with all her might . . . and at last I felt her weight on my back. She was safe!

She leaned forward, both hands buried in my mane and her legs shaking as they clung to my sides. All I had to do now was return her to dry land. I took my time, moving carefully across the shifting footing. Once or twice I felt Amma's balance waver. That was strange for Amma. Normally she rode with more grace than any other human I had known. But fighting the water had weakened her.

Each time she swayed and started to slip, I stopped short. I waited, as still as the mountains, until she found her balance again. Then I moved on, fighting the current with each step.

On the shore, people were gathered. Tassi was at the front, along with Amma's father and brothers. Everyone was shouting, but I hardly heard them. There was nothing they could do to help.

At last I felt the riverbed slope upward. One more step, then two, and the water was only as deep as my knees. Amma's father waded in to meet us. His arms reached for the girl, pulling her from my back and cradling her in his arms. She collapsed against his shoulder. Her bedraggled hair draped across his face, but he did not push it away.

He hurried back up the bank. Most of the other humans crowded around them, chattering anxiously in their human way.

I started up after them, my sides heaving.

Of all the many river crossings in my life, that had been the hardest.

Tassi came to me, putting a hand on my side as I clambered the rest of the way up the bank. I didn't need his help to make the climb. But it was nice to know that he was there.

"Good girl, Elska," he murmured when we reached the top. He rubbed my wet neck with both hands. "Good girl!"

The cold river water was clinging to me. I shook myself dry. The water showered out in all directions.

Tassi jumped back, shouting with laughter. "Bad girl, Elska!" he cried. But he did not sound angry.

Home

The birds were returning to Iceland. The snow cover had receded more than halfway up the mountains. The meadows were slowly changing from dry brown to green. Soon it would be time for the herd to return to the open highlands for the grazing season. The sheep were milling and bleating in their field. Even they understood what was coming.

It had been a long, cold, dark winter. I had worked hard, carrying messages and taking the boys fishing when the weather allowed. In the deepest part of the winter, of course, I had little to do. At those times, the humans rarely left home. But now they were busy again, preparing for the short growing season to come.

"Elska!" Amma burst into the yard, her pale hair flying behind her. "Are you ready to go?"

I nickered to her in greeting. It made me happy to see her every day. Ever since the day of the *rettir*, we had been together. I had returned to my home farm, my original herd, and my favorite human. Being there made the hardships—the harsh winter weather, the sometimes difficult work—much easier to bear.

Amma hugged me. "I'm going to miss you," she said into my shedding coat. "But at least now I know you'll come back to me in the autumn. I am so happy that Alfvaldr gifted you back to me!"

My ears pricked forward. Over Amma's shoulder, I could see that young Tassi had just ridden into the yard on a young dapple gray.

"Actually, my father didn't gift him to you, Amma. He gifted him back to your father," he called out.

Amma jumped in surprise, then turned and made a face at him. "Tassi! Were you listening to my private conversation with Elska?"

"It's not private if you speak loudly enough for every fish in the sea to hear," Tassi said, smiling broadly.

Amma tossed her head like a playful filly challenging a herdmate. "Well, it doesn't matter if you hear anyway. Elska is mine, and you know it!"

"True enough!" Tassi laughed. "But remember, you should be very nice to me, Amma. I was the one who convinced Father to trade her back to you in exchange for the buckskin mare." He laughed again. "Magni is still sour at losing his best racing horse!"

"I know." Amma scratched me under my mane. "But Alfvaldr told me he knew that Elska and I belonged together. He saw it when she rescued me from the river. How could he keep us apart after that?"

Tassi nodded. He slid down off his mount, then walked over and gave me a pat. "We miss Elska at home," he said. "But you're right. She belongs with you. Some things are meant to be."

Amma ducked her head against my neck. Then she turned and smiled at the human boy. He smiled back.

"Everybody ready to go?" Amma's brother

Valdi appeared in the yard at that moment. "It's getting late."

Tassi moved quickly away from Amma and me. "You're right, Valdi," he said, vaulting up onto his horse. "I'd better get home to help Father. I'll see you both later." With one last smile for Amma, he kicked his mount and rode away at a fast tölt.

Valdi watched him go. "What was young Tassi doing here?"

"I don't know." Amma busied herself untangling a knot in my mane. "I suppose he misses Elska and wanted to visit her."

"Yes. I'm sure it was Elska he wanted to see." Valdi chuckled. Then he moved on toward Jarpur, his usual mount. "All right, let's separate out the horses that are staying for the summer. Father will want to get the others off as soon as he comes out."

For the next few minutes, the two of them pulled horses from the herd and led them to a separate area. Hamur, Tyrta, Tappi, and others—each horse followed the humans willingly. All of us enjoyed the open, easy life spent grazing freely. But all of us were nearly as content to stay behind and help our human herdmates.

Finally Amma came back to me. "I wish you could stay, too, Elska," she said, scratching me again in all my favorite spots. "But Father says it is better if you go out this summer."

I rested my head against her shoulder. The sun was warm for so early in the season, and my eyes drifted half shut. In that moment, I was fully content.

Amma pushed aside my bushy forelock and looked into my eyes. "You will miss me, too, won't you?" Her voice was little more than a whisper, no louder than the arctic fox creeping among the dry grasses in a meadow. "But we will see each other again come autumn." She slipped back and rubbed my belly, which swelled more than usual for late winter. "By then you will have a foal to show me," Amma went on. "I can't wait to meet your baby, Elska dear. I know it will be just as special as you are. . . ."

horses to the island in boats along with other livestock. The harsh climate and challenging landscape helped mold the descendants of those horses into the hardy, sure-footed Icelandic breed of today.

The Bridges of Iceland

In the time of the Viking settlers and for many years after that, Iceland had few roads and even fewer bridges. Horses were expected to carry people through the varied terrain and across the many rivers. The lack of roads meant that the wheel did not come to Iceland until much later than most of the rest of the world, so horses were even more important there as work animals and as a means of transportation. Today the only traditional use still served primarily by the Icelandic horse is the annual *rettir*, or sheep roundup, which takes place each September, just as in Viking times. But many people throughout Iceland continue to keep horses for pleasure. And Icelandic horses have been exported to many other countries as well.

Short but No Pony

In most breeds, equines that stand 14.2 hands at the withers or shorter are considered ponies. But not Icelandics! Although they average around 13 to 14 hands, they are always properly referred to as horses, not ponies. Icelandics are very strong for their size and can carry more weight than many larger horses.

Gaits Like No Other

Icelandic horses are a gaited breed. All breeds of horse can perform three basic gaits: walk, trot, and canter/gallop. But gaited breeds have additional gaits. The Icelandics come with two extras—the tölt and the flying pace. The tölt is a comfortable, gliding gait, while the flying pace is a very fast gait used mostly for racing. Other gaited breeds, such as the Tennessee Walking Horse, the Five-Gaited Saddlebred, and the Missouri Foxtrotter, have their own varieties of these extra gaits.

Law of the Land

Even today, Icelandics are the only breed of horse in Iceland. In fact, it is forbidden by law to bring horses into the country. And if a horse leaves, it is not allowed to come back. This law has been in existence since around the year AD 900, which means that the Icelandic horse is considered one of the purest breeds in the world. The law has also protected the native Icelandic horse from many diseases that are common elsewhere.

A Colorful Bunch

Icelandics come in just about all possible equine colors. They also come in various pinto (spotted) patterns. In a herd of Icelandic horses, you might see several shades and patterns of chestnut, bay, black, gray, dun, buckskin, grullo, roan, silver dapple, palomino, and cremello, among others.

Safe and Sound

Icelandic horses have no natural predators in their homeland. This has helped give them an especially even, friendly temperament. Thanks to this, along with many years of selective breeding, they are generally less likely to be spooked than other breeds of horse. They are also very hardy and long-lived.

What's in a Name?

It is a tradition even today that most Icelandic horses are given an Icelandic name, even if they are bred elsewhere. Elska is an Icelandic name commonly used for mares; it means "friendly" or "playful."

MORE INTERESTING FACTS
ABOUT ICELAND

- There are almost no trees in Iceland.
- Like other extreme northern and southern areas, Iceland has very long days in the summer and very long nights in the winter.
- Iceland was created by volcanic activity and still has several active volcanoes.
- More than 10 percent of Iceland is covered by glaciers.
- The word *geyser* comes from the Icelandic language. There are lots of geysers in Iceland!
- Thanks to its volcanic and geothermal activity and its glaciers, Iceland is often

called the Land of Fire and Ice.

- Modern Icelanders are listed in their telephone book by first name.
- Geothermal energy is used for much of modern Iceland's heating and electricity. Icelanders even use it to heat some of their sidewalks!

Turn the page for a special preview
of the next Horse Diaries book.

HORSE DIARIES

Bell's Star

ALISON HART
illustrated by RUTH SANDERSON

AVAILABLE NOW!

Vermont, Early Spring 1850

I was born in a rocky paddock on a moon-less night. Light snow fell from the sky, covering my brown fur with white. My mother's tongue washed over me and warmed my skin. Soon she nudged me, urging me to stand.

Rise, she told me. *Danger can hide in the dark woods.*

I scrambled to my feet. My long legs were sturdy, my body stout. I nursed, and my mother's milk gave me strength. I hopped in the snow, trying out my legs. Mother smiled proudly as I trotted and leaped. Soon I grew weary, and sinking onto a soft pile of hay, I slept.

Morning came, and the rising sun broke through the clouds. As soon as it was light, my mother began to teach me.

There is so much to learn, she told me. I followed her around the paddock. She touched her nose to all the new things: *fence, tree, water trough, hay, mud.*

Mud I learned quickly. As the snow melted, my tiny hooves sank into the sloppy brown mess. I was scrambling onto a dry stump when a fluttering sound startled me.

A bright blue creature landed on the fence. I tensed. *Is this danger?* I asked my mother.

Her muzzle twitched in laughter. *No, my son. That is a blue jay. They are pesky and steal my corn, but they are not danger.*

Jumping off the stump, I whinnied to the blue jay. It flew into the trees.

Blue jays have wings, my mother explained. *They are free to fly to wherever they want.*

I peered between the fence rails. I wanted to race after the blue jay to the place called *wherever they want*. The blue jay had disappeared, but outside the paddock were many more new things to explore!

I touched my nose to the railing, but the fence circled my mother and me, penning us in. I checked my back. Did I have wings? All I saw was brown hair.

If only I had wings, I thought. *I could fly free, too.*

Suddenly a shriek filled the air. I fled behind my mother. I flicked my fuzzy ears. *Danger?* Turning, I peeked from beneath her thick black tail.

A creature leaped over the top railing, landing with a splash in the mud. It was as colorful and noisy as the blue jay, only bigger! Wings spread wide, it hurtled toward me.

Terrified, I turned to run, but my long legs tangled. I fell in a heap. Mud splattered my white star. The giant blue jay plopped on the ground next to me. Its wings wrapped tightly around my neck, and I was trapped!

Mother, I neighed. *Danger!*

But my mother's eyes were twinkling.

"Papa! Bell had her foal!" the blue jay cried out.

"I see, Miss Katie," an even taller blue jay answered. "But, daughter, your joy is scaring him. Let him go so we can see how fine he is."

The wings released me. I scrambled to my hooves and rushed to the far side of the paddock. My mother hurried after me and blew into my nostrils.

Do not be afraid. Those are humans. The large one is Papa. The small one is Katie. They feed and care for us. In return, we work for them.

Work. I did not know that word yet.

My mother pushed me forward. My legs splayed, refusing to move. The human called Papa set a wooden bucket in the paddock. "Come, Bell," he called. My mother trotted over. Dipping her head, she ate hungrily.

"You have given us a fine fellow, Bell," Papa said, patting her neck.

Wide-eyed and trembling, I stared at the human called Katie. She stood in the middle of the paddock, her eyes as curious as mine. Then she held out one wing.

This time she walked quietly to me. Her wings were soft when they stole around my neck. Then her cheek pressed against mine, and my trembling stopped.

"He has a white star, just like Bell," Katie said. "And look, two white legs."

"He's a fine-looking Morgan horse. Strong like his dam. Handsome like his sire," Papa said. "Soon he'll be able to pull the plow and the carriage."

"Papa, may I name him?" Katie asked.

He nodded.

"I name him Bell's Star."

"That's a grand name for such a small foal," Papa said.

"One day he *will* be grand, I know," Katie said, scratching my fuzzy mane. "He'll lead the St. Albans parade like Mr. Jones's Morgan horse."

"Let's hope he grows up to be as grand a worker as Bell," Papa said. "Our farm needs a Morgan that can pull a plow, not lead a parade."

I nuzzled Katie's arm. I didn't know *grand* or *parade*, but I wanted to show her I no longer thought she was *danger*.

"Oh, Papa," Katie sighed, her breath tickling my whiskers. "I love him already."

"We'll give Bell a day of rest," Papa said. "Then it's back to work tomorrow."

Work. There was that word again. That morning, with Katie's arms around my neck, I thought nothing more of it.

But soon I would know what it meant.

About the Author

Catherine Hapka has written more than 150 books for children and young adults, including many about horses. A lifelong horse lover, she rides several times a week and appreciates horses of all breeds. In addition to writing and riding, she enjoys all kinds of animals, reading, gardening, music, and travel. She lives on a small farm in Chester County, Pennsylvania, which she shares with a horse, three goats, a small flock of chickens, and too many cats.

About the Illustrator

Ruth Sanderson grew up with a love for horses. She drew them constantly, and her first oil painting at age fourteen was a horse portrait.

Ruth has illustrated and retold many fairy tales and likes to feature horses in them whenever possible. Her book about a magical horse, *The Golden Mare, the Firebird, and the Magic Ring,* won the Texas Bluebonnet Award in 2003. She illustrated the first Black Stallion paperback covers and has illustrated a number of chapter book horse stories, most recently *Summer Pony* and *Winter Pony* by Jean Slaughter Doty.

Ruth and her daughter have two horses, an Appaloosa named Thor and a quarter horse named Gabriel. She lives with her family in Massachusetts.

To find out more about her adventures with horses and the research she did to create the illustrations in this book, visit her Web site, www.ruthsanderson.com.

Collect all the books in the
Horse Diaries series!

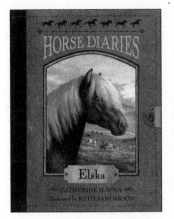

And coming soon